Directions to Servants

Directions to Servants

Jonathan Swift

ET REMOTISSIMA PROPE

100 PAGES

100 PAGES
Published by Hesperus Press Limited
4 Rickett Street, London SW6 1RU
www.hesperuspress.com

First published in 1745
First published by Hesperus Press Limited, 2003

Designed and typeset by Fraser Muggeridge
Printed in the United Arab Emirates by Oriental Press

ISBN: 1-84391-062-4

CONTENTS

Foreword by Colm Tóibín vii

Directions to Servants 1

Directions to:
- All Servants in General 3
- the Butler 13
- the Cook 25
- the Footman 32
- the Coachman 46
- the Groom 47
- the House Steward and Land Steward 53
- the Porter 54
- the Chambermaid 55
- the Waiting-maid 60
- the Housemaid 65
- the Dairymaid 68
- the Children's Maid 69
- the Nurse 70
- the Laundress 71
- the Housekeeper 72
- the Tutoress or Governess 73

Notes 74
Note on the text 75
Biographical note 77

FOREWORD

Jonathan Swift remained all of his life unsure of his own status. He was a master of invective and a lord of language and a controlling talent and a ruling wit, but in his constant seeking of preferment and promotion, in his uncertain relationship with a number of powerful men, his position was menial, and all the more painful for his hope and belief that it would not always be so. He was a faithful servant whose rage against his own servility caused him on occasion to lose, to his own detriment, all sense of caution. His peculiar imagination, in which the world can be set to rights only by being turned on its head, and in which reason and logic move naturally towards anarchy and nightmare, arose from the uneasy distance between his talent and his circumstances.

In the household of Sir William Temple where he had lived as a young man, his duties included reading aloud to his patron and keeping the household accounts. Temple's nephew, who did not like him, later insisted that Swift was not allowed to sit at table with the family. Swift's 'bitterness, satire, moroseness' made him 'insufferable both to equals and inferiors, and unsafe for his superiors to countenance', the nephew said. It is unclear whether this was entirely accurate, but the fact that it could be later used as a way of undermining Swift serves to emphasise how vulnerable a position a brilliant and resentful young man with neither tact nor fortune held in such houses.

Swift the solitary bachelor knew a great deal about servants. He allowed them to become a mock-family and a source of much exasperation and amusement. 'I am plagued to death with turning away and taking servants,' he wrote when he became Dean of St Patrick's in Dublin. He read prayers to his 'family', as he often called them, 'at a fixed hour every night in his own bedchamber'. In Dublin in 1715, when his friends in London had been disgraced and his personal life had become too complicated, he saw no one else. 'I live in a corner of a vast unfurnished house; my family consists of a steward, a groom, a helper in the stable, a footman, and an old maid, who are all at board wages.' His new cook whom he called 'Sweetheart', he wrote, was 'as old and ugly' as her predecessor, 'for the ladies of my acquaintance would not allow me one with a tolerable face though I most earnestly interceded for it'. In 1722, when Saunders, one of his servants, died, Swift wrote that he was 'one of my best friends as well as the best servant in the kingdom'. He erected a monument to him in St Patrick's. On the other hand, Patrick, another servant, who made cameo appearances in Swift's letters to Stella, got drunk three times a week and, once, when he disappeared with the key and returned drunk, Swift had no choice but to give him 'two or three swingeing cuffs on the ear, and I have strained the thumb on my left hand with pulling him'.

In the middle of all his savage indignation, his efforts to solicit support from the powerful, his whinings and his prayers with his servants, Swift was hilariously funny. He combined a great schoolboy feeling for jokes about toilets and matters of hygiene with the joy of slapstick and with the pleasure, which made him enemies and many friends, of taking the joke too far so that laughter brought not only tears but a permanent disrespect for both elders and betters. Dr Johnson took the view that the many details in *Directions to Servants*, which was first published in 1731 but begun much earlier, possibly as early as 1704, must have been noted down over many years 'for such a number of particulars could never have been assembled by the power of recollection'.

'With Swift comes the voice,' Elizabeth Bowen wrote, in a review of a book about the emergence of the Anglo-Irish. 'The dooming,' as she put it, 'of the English Dean to become never quite an Irishman but an Irish patriot' offered him a tone which moved beyond the wit of his English contemporaries. In Ireland he learnt to hate his neighbour as himself and then write accordingly; the English language in Dublin could be both a route to power and an accent to mimic; it was for Swift both sweet and malicious. Yeats, in an essay on Swift, quoted Goldsmith, writing 'that he had never laughed so much at Garrick's acting as at somebody in an Irish tavern mimicking a Quaker sermon'. Thus *Directions to Servants* reads as a central document in the long, comic and sly history of Irish disrespect which includes Sterne and Sheridan and Wilde, Joyce and Beckett and Flann O'Brien.

This tradition depends not on the originality of the argument or indeed the quality of the wit, but on the lengths the creator is prepared to go to play off the monotony of a rule book, say, or the plainness of an ordinary day, against the sheer energy of the sentences in their dynamic structure and tone, the quality of minute observation, the cheeky choice of detail. 'Never send up a leg of a fowl at supper,' Swift advised his cook in *Directions to Servants*, 'while there is a cat or a dog in the house that can be accused for running off with it.' So far so good, and reasonable and nicely subversive, but it is in the next sentence that Swift's reason most wonderfully loses the run of itself. 'But if there happen to be neither, you must lay it upon the rats or a strange greyhound.' That strange greyhound, helped along by the rats, comes to snatch the sentence from the dull and worthy jaws of satire and gobble it up in a feast of mystery and unreason. It is a stroke of genius with which so many of the sentences in *Directions to Servants* abound. This makes the work not only a cause of vast and unending entertainment, but, in the final analysis, worthy of detailed study and, indeed, worth heeding, even in the most humble households, and on all sides of the Irish Sea, down to the letter.

– Colm Tóibín, 2003

Directions to Servants

Directions to All Servants in General

When your master or lady call a servant by name, if that servant be not in the way, none of you are to answer, for then there will be no end of your drudgery, and masters themselves allow that if a servant comes when he is called it is sufficient.

When you have done a fault, be always pert and insolent, and behave yourself as if you were the injured person; this will immediately put your master or lady off their mettle.

If you see your master wronged by any of your fellow-servants, be sure to conceal it, for fear of being called a telltale. However, there is one exception, in the case of a favourite servant, who is justly hated by the whole family – who therefore are bound in prudence to lay all the faults they can upon the favourite.

The cook, the butler, the groom, the market-man, and every other servant who is concerned in the expenses of the family should act as if his master's whole estate ought to be applied to that servant's particular business. For instance, if the cook computes his master's estate to be a thousand pounds a year, he reasonably concludes that a thousand pounds a year will afford meat enough, and, therefore, he need not be saving; the butler makes the same judgement, so may the groom and the coachman, and thus every branch of expense will be filled to your master's honour.

Whenever you are chided before company (which, with submission to our masters and ladies, is an unmannerly practice), it often happens that some stranger will have the good nature to drop a word in your excuse; in such a case you have a good title to justify yourself, and may rightly conclude that whenever he chides you afterwards or on other occasions, he may be in the wrong, in which opinion you will be the better confirmed by stating the case to your fellow-servants in your own way, who will certainly decide in your favour. Therefore, as I have said before, whenever you are chided, complain as if you were injured.

It often happens that servants sent on messages, are apt to stay out somewhat longer than the message requires, perhaps two, four, six, or eight hours, or some such trifle; for the temptation to be sure was great, and flesh and blood cannot always resist. When you return, the master storms, the lady scolds, stripping, cudgelling and turning off is the word. But here you ought to be provided with a set of excuses, enough to serve on all occasions: for instance, your uncle came fourscore miles to town this morning, on purpose to see you, and goes back by break of day tomorrow; a brother-servant, that borrowed money of you when he was out of place, was running away to Ireland; you were taking leave of an old fellow-servant, who was shipping for Barbados; your father sent an old cow for you to sell, and you could not find a chapman till nine at night; you were taking leave of a dear cousin who is to be hanged next Saturday; you wrenched your foot against a stone, and were forced to stay three hours in a shop, before you could stir a step; some nastiness was thrown on you out of a garret window, and you were ashamed to come home before you were cleaned and the smell went off; you were pressed for the sea-service, and carried before a justice of the peace, who kept you three hours before he examined you, and you got off with much ado; a bailiff by mistake seized you for a debtor, and kept you the whole evening in a sponging house[1]; you were told your master had gone to a tavern, and come to some mischance, and your grief was so great that you enquired for his honour in a hundred taverns between Pall Mall and Temple Bar.

Take all tradesmen's parts against your master, and when you are sent to buy anything, never offer to cheapen it, but generously pay the full demand. This is highly for your master's honour, and may be some shillings in your pocket; and you are to consider if your master hath paid too much, he can better afford the loss than a poor tradesman.

Never submit to stir a finger in any business but that for which you were particularly hired. For example, if the groom be drunk or absent, and the butler be ordered to shut the stable door, the answer is ready, 'An please, Your Honour, I don't understand horses'; if a corner of the hanging wants a single nail to fasten it, and the footman be directed to tack it up, he may say he doth not understand that sort of work, but His Honour may send for the upholsterer.

Masters and ladies are usually quarrelling with the servants for not shutting the doors after them, but neither masters nor ladies consider that those doors must be open before they can be shut, and that the labour is double to open and shut the doors; therefore the best, the shortest, and easiest way is to do neither. But if you are so often teased to shut the door that you cannot easily forget it, then give the door such a clap as you go out, as will shake the whole room, and make everything rattle in it, to put your master and lady in mind that you observe their directions.

If you find yourself to grow into favour with your master or lady, take some opportunity, in a very mild way, to give them warning; and when they ask the reason, and seem loath to part with you, answer that you would rather live with them than anybody else, but a poor servant is not to be blamed if he strives to better himself, that service is no inheritance, that your work is great, and your wages very small; upon which, if your master hath any generosity, he will add five or ten shillings a quarter rather than let you go. But if you are baulked, and have no mind to go off, get some fellow-servant to tell your master that he hath prevailed upon you to stay.

Whatever good bits you can pilfer in the day, save them to junket with your fellow-servants at night, and take in the butler, provided he will give you drink.

Write your own name and your sweetheart's with the smoke of a candle on the roof of the kitchen, or the servants' hall, to show your learning.

If you are a young, sightly fellow, whenever you whisper your mistress at the table, run your nose full in her cheek, or if your breath be good, breathe full in her face; this I know to have had very good consequences in some families.

Never come till you have been called three or four times, for none but dogs will come at the first whistle; and when the master calls, 'Who's there?' no servant is bound to come, for *Who's there* is nobody's name.

When you have broken all your earthen drinking vessels below stairs (which is usually done in a week) the copper pot will do as well; it can boil milk, heat porridge, hold small beer, or in case of necessity serve for a jordan[2]. Therefore apply it indifferently to all these uses, but never wash or scour it, for fear of taking off the tin.

Although you are allowed knives for the servants' hall at meals, yet you ought to spare them, and make use only of your master's.

Let it be a constant rule that no chair, stool or table in the servants' hall or the kitchen shall have above three legs, which hath been the ancient and constant practice in all the families I ever knew, and is said to be founded upon two good reasons: first, to show that servants are ever in a tottering condition;

secondly, it was thought a point of humility that the servants' chairs and tables should have at least one leg fewer than those of their masters. I grant there hath been an exception to this rule with regard to the cook, who by old custom was allowed an easy chair to sleep in after dinner, and yet I have seldom seen them with above three legs. Now this epidemical lameness of servants is by philosophers attributed to two causes, which are observed to make the greatest revolutions in states and empires: I mean love and war. A stool, a chair, or a table is the first weapon taken up in a general romping or skirmish; and after a peace, the chairs, if they be not very strong, are apt to suffer in the conduct of an amour – the cook being usually fat and heavy, and the butler a little in drink.

I could never endure to see maidservants so ungenteel as to walk the streets with their petticoats pinned up. It is a foolish excuse to allege their petticoats will be dirty, when they have so easy a remedy as to walk three or four times down a clean pair of stairs after they come home.

When you stop to tattle with some crony servant in the same street, leave your own street door open, that you may get in without knocking when you come back, otherwise your mistress may know you are gone out, and you will be chided.

I do most earnestly exhort you all to unanimity and concord. But mistake me not, you may quarrel with each other as much as you please, only bear in mind that you have a common enemy, which is your master and lady, and you have a common cause to defend. Believe an old practitioner: whoever, out of malice to a fellow-servant, carries a tale to his master shall be ruined by a general confederacy against him.

The general place of rendezvous for all servants, both in winter and summer, is the kitchen; there the grand affairs of the family ought to be consulted, whether they concern the stable, the dairy, the pantry, the laundry, the cellar, the nursery, the dining room, or my lady's chamber; there, as in your own proper element, you can laugh and squall and romp in full security.

When any servant comes home drunk, and cannot appear, you must all join in telling your master that he is gone to bed very sick, upon which your lady will be so good-natured as to order some comfortable thing for the poor man or maid.

When your master and lady go abroad together to dinner, or on a visit for the evening, you need leave only one servant in the house, unless you have a blackguard-boy to answer at the door and attend the children, if there be any. Who is to stay at home is to be determined by short and long cuts, and the stayer at home may be comforted by a visit from a sweetheart, without danger of being caught together. These opportunities must never be missed, because they come but sometimes, and all is safe enough while there is a servant in the house.

When your master or lady comes home, and wants a servant who happens to be abroad, your answer must be that he is but just that minute stepped out, being sent for by a cousin who is dying.

If your master calls you by name, and you happen to answer at the fourth call, you need not hurry yourself; and if you be chided for staying, you may lawfully say you came no sooner, because you did not know what you were called for.

When you are chided for a fault, as you go out of the room and downstairs, mutter loud enough to be plainly heard; this will make him believe you are innocent.

Whoever comes to visit your master or lady when they are abroad, never burden your memory with the person's name, for indeed you have too many other things to remember.

Besides, it is a porter's business, and your master's fault that he does not keep one, and who can remember names? And you will certainly mistake them, and you can neither write nor read.

If it be possible, never tell a lie to your master or lady, unless you have some hopes that they cannot find it out in less than half an hour. When a servant is turned off, all his faults must be told, although most of them were never known by his master or lady, and all mischiefs done by others, charged to him. (Instance them.) And when they ask any of you why you never acquainted them before, the answer is: 'Sir, or madam, really I was afraid it would make you angry, and besides perhaps you might think it was malice in me.' Where there are little masters and misses in a house, they are usually great impediments to the diversions of the servants; the only remedy is to bribe them with goody-goodies, that they may not tell tales to Papa and Mamma.

I advise you of the servants whose master lives in the country, and who expect vails[3], always to stand rank and file when a stranger is taking his leave, so that he must of necessity pass between you; and he must have more confidence, or less money, than usual if any of you let him escape, and, according as he behaves himself, remember to treat him the next time he comes.

If you are sent with ready money to buy anything at a shop, and happen at that time to be out of pocket (which is very usual) sink the money and take up the goods on your master's account. This is for the honour of your master and yourself, for he becomes a man of credit at your recommendation.

When your lady sends for you up to her chamber to give you any orders, be sure to stand at the door and keep it open, fiddling with the lock all the while she is talking to you, and keep the button in your hand for fear you should forget to shut the door after you.

If your master or lady happen once in their lives to accuse you wrongfully, you are a happy servant, for you have nothing more to do than for every fault you commit, while you are in their service, to put them in mind of that false accusation, and protest yourself equally innocent in the present case.

When you have a mind to leave your master, and are too bashful to break the matter for fear of offending him, your best way is to grow rude and saucy of a sudden, and beyond your usual behaviour, till he finds it necessary to turn you off; and when you are gone, to revenge yourself, give him and his lady such a character to all your brother-servants who are out of place, that none will venture to offer their service.

Some nice ladies who are afraid of catching cold, having observed that the maids and fellows below stairs often forget to shut the door after them as they come in or go out into the backyards, have contrived that a pulley and rope, with a large piece of lead at the end, should be fixed as to make the door shut of itself, and require a strong hand to open it, which is an immense toil to servants, whose business may force them to go in and out fifty times in a morning. But ingenuity can do much, for prudent servants have found out an effectual remedy against this insupportable grievance, by tying up the pulley in such a manner that the weight of the lead will have no effect; however, as to my part, I would rather choose to keep the door always open by laying a heavy stone at the bottom of it.

The servants' candlesticks are generally broken, for nothing can last for ever, but you may find out many expedients: you may conveniently stick your candle in a bottle, or with a lump of butter against the wainscot, in a powder-horn, or in an old shoe, or in a cleft stick, or in the barrel of a pistol, in a coffee cup or a drinking glass, a horn can, a teapot, a twisted napkin, a mustard pot, an inkhorn, a marrowbone, a piece of dough, or you may cut a hole in a loaf and stick it in there.

When you invite the neighbouring servants to junket with you at home in an evening, teach them a particular way of tapping or scraping at the kitchen window, which you may hear, but not your master or lady, whom you must take care not to disturb or frighten at such unseasonable hours.

Lay all faults on a lap dog, a favourite cat, a monkey, a parrot, a magpie, a child, or on the servant who was last turned off; by this rule you will excuse yourself, do no hurt to anybody else, and save your master or lady from the trouble and vexation of chiding.

When you want proper instruments for any work you are about, use all expedients you can invent rather than leave your work undone. For instance, if the poker be out of the way or broken, stir up the fire with the tongs; if the tongs are not at hand, use the muzzle of the bellows, the wrong end of the fire shovel, the handle of the fire brush, the end of a mop, or your master's cane. If you want paper to singe a fowl, tear the first book you see about the house. Wipe your shoes for want of a clout, with the bottom of a curtain, or a damask napkin. Strip your livery lace for garters. If the butler wants a jordan, in case of need, he may use the great silver cup.

There are several ways of putting out candles, and you ought to be instructed in them all: you may run the candle end against the wainscot, which puts the snuff out immediately; you may lay it on the floor and tread the snuff out with your foot; you may hold it upside down until it is choked with its own grease; or cram it into the socket of the candlestick; you may whirl it round in your hand till it goes out; when you go to bed, after you have made water, you may dip your candle end into the chamber pot; you may spit on your finger and thumb, and pinch the snuff until it goes out; the cook may run the candle's nose into the meal tub, or the groom into a vessel of oats, or a lock of hay, or a heap of litter; the housemaid may put out her candle by running it against a looking glass, which nothing cleans so well as candle snuff; but the quickest and best of all methods is to blow it out with your breath, which leaves the candle clear and readier to be lighted.

There is nothing so pernicious in a family as a telltale, against whom it must be the principal business of you all to unite; whatever office he serves in, take all opportunities to spoil the business he is about and to cross him in everything. For instance, if the butler be the telltale, break his glasses whenever he leaves the pantry open, or lock the cat or the mastiff in it, who will do as well; mislay a fork or a spoon, so he may never find it. If it be the cook, whenever she turns her back, throw a lump of soot or a handful of salt in the pot, or smoking coals into the dripping-pan, or daub the roast meat with the back of the chimney, or hide the key of the jack. If a footman be suspected, let the cook daub the back of his new livery, or, when he is going up with a dish of soup, let her follow him softly with a ladleful, and dribble it all the way upstairs to the dining room, and then let the housemaid make such a noise that her lady may hear it. The waiting-maid is very likely to be guilty of this fault, in hopes to ingratiate herself. In this case, the laundress must be sure to tear her smocks in the washing, and yet wash them but half; and when she complains, tell all the house that she sweats so much and her flesh is so nasty that she fouls a smock more in one hour than the kitchen-maid doth in a week.

Directions to the Butler

In my directions to servants, I find from my long observation that you, butler, are the principal party concerned.

Your business being of the greatest variety, and requiring the greatest exactness, I shall, as well as I can recollect, run through the several branches of your office, and order my instructions accordingly.

In waiting at the sideboard, take all possible care to save your own trouble, and your master's drink and glasses. Therefore, first, since those who dine at the same table are supposed to be friends, let them all drink out of the same glass without washing, which will save you much pains, as well as the hazard of breaking them. Give no person any liquor till he has called for it thrice at least, by which means, some out of modesty, and others out of forgetfulness, will call the seldomer, and thus your master's liquor be saved.

If anyone desires a glass of bottled ale, first shake the bottle to see whether anything be in it, then taste it to know what liquor it is, that you may not be mistaken, and lastly wipe the mouth of the bottle with the palm of your hand to show your cleanliness.

Be more careful to have the cork in the belly of the bottle than in the mouth, and if the cork be musty, or white friars[4] in your liquor, your master will save the more.

If a humble companion, a chaplain, a tutor, or a dependent cousin happen to be at table, whom you find to be little regarded by the master and the company, which nobody is readier to discover and observe than we servants, it must be the business of you and the footman to follow the example of your betters by treating him many degrees worse than any of the rest; and you cannot please your master better, or at least your lady.

If anyone calls for small beer towards the end of dinner, do not give yourself the pains of going down to the cellar, but gather the droppings and leavings out of the several cups and glasses and salvers into one – but turn your back on the company, for fear of being observed. On the contrary, if anyone calls for ale towards the end of dinner, fill the largest tankard top-full, by which you will have the greatest part left to oblige your fellow-servants without the sin of stealing from your master.

There is likewise an honest perquisite by which you have a chance of getting every day the best part of a bottle of wine to yourself, for you are not to suppose that gentlefolks will value the remainder of a bottle; therefore, always set a fresh one before them after dinner, although there hath not been above one glass drunk of the other.

Take special care that your bottles be not musty before you fill them, in order to which, blow strongly into the mouth of every bottle, and then if you smell nothing but your own breath, immediately fill it.

If you are sent down in haste to draw any drink, and find it will not run, do not be at the trouble of opening a vent, but blow strongly into the fosset, and you will find it immediately pour into your mouth; or take out the vent, but do not stay to put it in again, for fear your master should want you.

If you are curious to taste some of your master's choice bottles, empty as many of them just below the neck as will make the quantity you want, but then take care to fill them up again with clean water, that you may not lessen your master's liquor.

There is an excellent invention found out of late years in the management of ale and small beer at the sideboard: for instance, a gentleman calls for a glass of ale and drinks but half, another calls for small beer – you immediately teem out the remainder of the ale into the tankard and fill the glass with small beer, and so backwards and forwards as long as dinner lasts, by which you answer three great ends: first, you save yourself the trouble of washing, and consequently the danger of breaking your glasses; secondly, you are sure not to be mistaken in giving gentlemen the liquor they call for; and lastly, by this method you are certain that nothing is lost.

Because butlers often forget to bring up their ale and beer time enough, be sure you remember to have up yours two hours before dinner, and place them in the sunny part of the room to let people see that you have not been negligent.

Some butlers have a way of decanting (as they call it) bottled ale, by which they lose a good part of the bottom; let your method be to turn the bottle directly upside down, which will make the liquor appear double the quantity. By this means, you will be sure not to lose one drop, and the froth will conceal the muddiness.

Clean your plate, wipe your knives and rub the foul table with the napkins and the tablecloth used that day, for it is but one washing; besides you save wearing out the coarse rubbers, in reward of which good husbandry, my judgement is that you may lawfully make use of the finest damask napkins to be nightcaps for yourself.

When you clean your plate, leave the whiting plainly to be seen in all the chinks, for fear your lady should believe you had not cleaned it.

There is nothing wherein the skill of a butler more appears than the management of candles, whereof, although some part may fall to the share of other servants, yet you being the principal person concerned, I shall direct my instructions upon this article to you only, leaving your fellow-servants to apply them upon occasion.

First, to avoid burning daylight and to save your master's candles, never bring them up until half an hour after it be dark, although they be called for ever so often.

Let your sockets be full of grease to the brim, with the old snuff at the top, then stick on your fresh candles. It is true, this may endanger their falling, but the candles will appear so much the longer and handsomer before company. At other times, for variety, put your candles loose in the sockets to show they are clean to the bottom.

When your candle is too big for the socket, melt it to a right size in the fire; and to hide the smut, wrap in paper halfway up.

You cannot but observe the great extravagance of late years among the gentry upon the article of candles, which a good butler ought by all means to discourage, both to save his own pains and his master's money. This may be contrived several ways, as when you are ordered to put candles into the sconces.

Sconces are great wasters of candles, and you, who are always to consider the advantage of your master, should do your utmost to discourage them. Therefore, your business must be to press the candle with both your hands into the socket, so as to make it lean in such a manner that the grease may drop all upon the floor, if some lady's headdress or gentleman's periwig be not ready to intercept it. You may likewise stick the candle so loose that it will fall upon the glass of the sconce and break it into shatters; this will save your master many a fair penny in the year, both in candles and to the glassman, and yourself much labour, for the sconces spoilt cannot be used.

Never let the candles burn too low, but give them as a lawful perquisite to your friend the cook, to increase her kitchen-stuff, or if this not be allowed in your house, give them in charity to the poor neighbours, who often run on your errands.

When you cut bread for a toast, do not stand idly watching it, but lay it on the coals and mind your other business; then come back, and if you find it toasted quite through, scrape off the burnt side, and serve it up.

When you dress up your sideboard, set the best glasses as near the edge of the table as you can, by which means they will cast a double lustre and make a much finer figure, and the consequence can be at worst but the breaking of half a dozen, which is a trifle in your master's pocket.

Wash the glasses with your own water to save your master's salt.

When any salt is spilt on the table, do not let it be lost, but when dinner is done, fold up the tablecloth with the salt in it, then shake the salt out into the salt cellar to serve next day; but the shortest and surest way is, when you remove the cloth, to wrap the knives, forks, spoons, salt cellars, broken bread and scraps all together in the tablecloth, by which you will be sure to lose nothing, unless you think it better to shake them out of the window among the beggars, that they may with more convenience eat the scraps.

Leave the dregs of ale, wine and other liquors in the bottles; to rinse them is but loss of time, since all will be done at once in a general washing, and you will have a better excuse for breaking them.

If your master hath many musty, or very foul and crusted bottles, I advise you, in point of conscience, that those may be the first you truck at the next alehouse for ale or brandy.

When a message is sent to your master, be kind to your brother-servant who brings it; give him the best liquor in your keeping, for your master's honour, and with the first opportunity he will do the same to you.

After supper, if it be dark, carry your plate and china together in the same basket to save candlelight, for you know your pantry well enough to put them up in the dark.

When company is expected at dinner, or in evenings, be sure to be abroad, that nothing may be got which is under your key, by which your master will save his liquor and not wear out his plate.

I come now to a most important part of your economy, the bottling of a hogshead of wine, wherein I recommend three virtues: cleanliness, frugality and brotherly love. Let your corks be of the longest kind you can get, which will save some wine in the neck of every bottle. As to your bottles, choose the smallest you can find, which will increase the number of dozens and please your master, for a bottle of wine is always a bottle of wine, whether it hold more or less, and if your master hath his proper number of dozens he cannot complain.

Every bottle must first be rinsed with wine, for fear of any moisture left in the washing; some out of mistaken thrift will rinse a dozen bottles with the same wine, but I would advise you for more caution to change the wine at every second bottle. A gill may be enough. Have bottles ready by to save it, and it will be a good perquisite, either to sell or drink with the cook.

Never draw your hogshead too low, nor tilt it for fear of disturbing the liquor. When it begins to run slow, and before the wine grows cloudy, shake the hogshead and carry a glass of it to your master, who will praise your discretion and give you all the rest as a perquisite of your place; you may tilt the hogshead the next day, and in a fortnight get a dozen or two of good clear wine to dispose of as you please.

In bottling wine, fill your mouth full of corks, together with a large plug of tobacco, which will give to the wine the true taste of the weed, so delightful to all good judges in drinking.

When you are ordered to decant a suspicious bottle, if a pint be out, give your hand a dextrous shake and show it in a glass, that it begins to be muddy.

When a hogshead of wine or any other liquor is to be bottled off, wash your bottles immediately before you begin, but be sure not to drain them, by which good management your master will save some gallons in every hogshead.

This is the time that, in honour to your master, you ought to show your kindness to your fellow-servants, and especially to the cook. What signifies a few flagons out of a whole hogshead? But make them be drunk in your presence, for fear they should be given to other folks, and so your master be wronged; but advise them, if they get drunk, to go to bed and leave word they are sick, which last caution I would have all the servants observe, both male and female.

If your master finds the hogshead to fall short of his expectation, what is plainer than that the vessel leaked; that the wine cooper had not filled it in proper time; that the merchant cheated him with a hogshead below the common measure?

When you are to get water on for tea after dinner (which in many families is part of your office), to save firing and to make more haste, pour it into the tea-kettle from the pot where cabbage or fish have been boiling, which will make it much wholesomer by curing the acid, corroding quality of the tea.

Be saving of your candles, and let those in the sconces, the hall, the stairs and in the lantern burn down into the sockets until they go out of themselves, for which your master and lady will commend your thriftiness, as soon as they shall smell the snuffs.

If a gentleman leaves his snuffbox or toothpick-case on the table after dinner and goes away, look upon it as part of your vails, for so it is allowed by all servants, and you do no wrong to your master or lady.

If you serve a country squire, when gentlemen and ladies come to dine at your house, never fail to make their servants drunk, and especially the coachman, for the honour of your master, to which, in all your actions, you must have a special regard, as being the best judge; for the honour of every family is deposited in the hands of the cook, the butler and the groom, as I shall hereafter demonstrate.

Snuff the candles at supper as they stand on the table, which is much the securest way, because, if the burning snuff happens to get out of the snuffers, you have a chance that it may fall into a dish of soup, sack-posset, rice-milk or the like, where it will be immediately extinguished with very little stink.

When you have snuffed the candle, always leave the snuffers open, for then the snuff will of itself burn away to ashes, and cannot fall out and dirty the table when you snuff the candles again.

That the salt may lie smooth in the salt-cellar, press it down with your moist palm.

When a gentleman is going away after dining with your master, be sure to stand full in his view and follow him to the door, and, as you have opportunity, look him full in the face; perhaps it may bring you a shilling, but if the gentleman hath lain there a night, get the cook, the housemaid, the stablemen, the scullion and the gardener to accompany you and to stand in his way to the hall, in a line on each side him; if the gentleman performs handsomely, it will do him honour and cost your master nothing.

You need not wipe your knife to cut bread for the table; in cutting a slice or two it will wipe itself.

Put your finger into every bottle to feel whether it be full, which is the surest way, for feeling hath no fellow.

When you go down to the cellar to draw ale or small beer, take care to observe directly the following method. Hold the vessel between the finger and thumb of your right hand, with the palm upwards, then hold the candle between your fingers, but a little leaning towards the mouth of the vessel, then take out the spiggot with your left hand and clap the point of it in your mouth, and keep your left hand to watch accidents. When the vessel is full, withdraw the spiggot from your mouth, well wetted with spittle, which being of a slimy consistence will make it stick faster in the fosset. If any tallow drops into the vessel you may easily (if you think of it) remove it with a spoon, or rather with your finger.

Always lock up a cat in the closet where you keep your china plates, for fear the mice may steal in and break them.

A good butler always breaks off the point of his bottle-screw in two days, by trying which is harder, the point of the screw or the neck of the bottle; in this case, to supply the want of a screw, after the stump hath torn the cork in pieces, make use of a silver fork, and when the scraps of the cork are almost drawn out, flirt the mouth of the bottle into the cistern three or four times, until you quite clear it.

If a gentleman dines often with your master, and gives you nothing when he goes away, you may use several methods to show him some marks of your displeasure and quicken his memory: if he calls for bread or drink, you may pretend not to hear, or send it to another who called after him; if he asks for wine, let him stay awhile, and then send him small beer; give him always foul glasses; send him a spoon when he wants a knife; wink at the footman to leave him without a plate. By these and the like expedients, you may probably be a better man by half a crown before he leaves the house, provided you watch an opportunity of standing by when he is going.

If your lady loves play, your fortune is fixed for ever: moderate gaming will be a perquisite of ten shillings a week, and in such a family I would rather choose to be butler than chaplain, or even rather than be steward. It is all ready money and got without labour, unless your lady happens to be one of those who either obligeth you to find wax candles or forceth you to divide it with some favourite servants, but, at worst, the old cards are your own, and if the gamesters pay deep or grow peevish, they will change the cards so often that the old ones will be a considerable advantage by selling them off to coffee houses, or families who love play but cannot afford better than cards at second hand. When you attend at this service, be sure to leave new packs within the reach of the gamesters, which those who have ill luck will readily take to change their fortune, and now and then an old pack mingled with the rest will easily pass. Be sure to be very officious on play nights, and ready with your candles to light out your company, and have salvers of wine at hand to give them when they call; but manage so with the cook that there be no supper, because it will be so much saved in your master's family, and because a supper will considerably lessen your gains.

Next to cards, there is nothing so profitable to you as bottles, in which perquisite you have no competitors except the footmen, who are apt to steal and vend them for pots of beer, but you are bound to prevent any such abuses in your master's family. The footmen are not to answer for what are broken at a general bottling, and those may be as many as your discretion will make them.

The profit of glasses is so very inconsiderable that it is hardly worth mentioning; it consists only in a small present made by the glass-man, and about four shillings in the pound added to the prices for your trouble and skill in choosing them. If your master hath a large stock of glasses, and you or your fellow-servants happen to break any of them without your master's knowledge, keep it a secret until there are not enough left to serve the table, then tell the master that the glasses are gone; this will be but one vexation to him, which is much better than fretting once or twice a week, and it is the office of a good servant to discompose his master and his lady as seldom as he can, and here the cat and dog will be of great use to take the blame from you. *Note:* that bottles missing are supposed to be half stolen by stragglers and other servants, and the other half broken by accident and at a general washing.

Whet the backs of your knives until they are as sharp as the edge, which will have this advantage, that when gentlemen find them blunt on one side, they may try the other; and to show you spare no pains in sharpening the knives, whet them so long till you wear out a good part of the iron and even the bottom of the silver handle. This doth credit to your master, for it shows good housekeeping, and the goldsmith may one day make you a present.

Your lady, when she finds the small beer or ale dead, will blame you for not remembering to put the peg into the vent hole. This is a great mistake, nothing being plainer than that the peg keeps the air in the vessel, which spoils the drink, and therefore ought to be let out, but if she insisteth upon it, to prevent the trouble of pulling out the vent and putting it in a dozen times a day, which is not to be borne by a good servant, leave the spiggot half out at night, and you will find, with only the loss of two or three quarts of liquor, the vessel will run freely.

When you prepare your candles, wrap them up in a piece of brown paper, and so stick them in the socket; let the paper come halfway up the candle, which looks handsome if anybody should come in.

Do all in the dark (as clean glasses, etc.) to save your master's candles.

Directions to the Cook

Although I am not ignorant that it hath been a long time since the custom began among people of quality to keep men cooks, and generally of the French nation, yet because my treatise is chiefly calculated for the general run of knights, squires and gentlemen, both in town and country, I shall therefore apply to you, Mrs Cook, as a woman. However, a great part of what I intend may serve for either sex, and your part naturally follows the former, because the butler and you are joined in interest. Your vails are generally equal, and paid when others are disappointed. You can junket together at nights upon your own prog[5], when the rest of the house are abed, and have it in your power to make every fellow-servant your friend. You can give a good bit or a good sup to the little masters and misses and gain their affections. A quarrel between you is very dangerous to you both, and will probably end in one of you being turned off, in which fatal case, perhaps, it will not be so easy in some time to cotton with another. And now, Mrs Cook, I proceed to give you my instructions, which I desire you will get some fellow-servant in the family to read to you constantly one night in every week upon your going to bed, whether you serve in town or country, for my lessons shall be fitted to both.

If your lady forgets at supper that there is any cold meat in the house, do not you be so officious as to put her in mind; it is plain she did not want it and, if she recollects it the next day, say she gave you no orders and it is spent; therefore, for fear of telling a lie, dispose of it with the butler, or any other crony, before you go to bed.

Never send up a leg of a fowl at supper while there is a cat or a dog in the house that can be accused for running off with it.

But if there happen to be neither, you must lay it upon the rats or a strange greyhound.

It is ill housewifery to foul your kitchen rubbers with wiping the bottoms of the dishes you send up, since the tablecloth will do as well, and is changed every meal.

Never clean your spits after they have been used, for the grease left upon them by meat is the best thing to preserve them from rust, and when you make use of them again, the same grease will make the inside of the meat moist.

If you live in a rich family, roasting and boiling are below the dignity of your office, and which it becomes you to be ignorant of, therefore leave that work wholly to the kitchen-wench, for fear of disgracing the family you live in.

If you be employed in marketing, buy your meat as cheap as you can, but when you bring in your accounts, be tender of your master's honour and set down the highest rate, which besides is but justice, for nobody can afford to sell at the same rate he buys, and I am confident that you may always safely swear that you gave no more than what the butcher and poulterer asked. If your lady orders you to set up a piece of meat for supper, you are not to understand that you must set it up *all*, therefore you may give half to yourself and the butler.

Good cooks cannot abide what they very justly call fiddling work, where abundance of time is spent and little done. Such, for instance, is the dressing small birds, requiring a world of cookery and clutter and a second or third spit, which, by the way, is absolutely needless, for it would be a very ridiculous thing indeed if a spit which is strong enough to turn a sirloin of beef should not be able to turn a lark. However, if your lady be nice, and is afraid that a large spit will tear them, place them handsomely in the dripping-pan, where the fat of roasted mutton or beef falling on the birds will serve to baste them, and so save both time and butter; for what cook of any spirit would lose her time in picking larks, wheatears and other small birds, therefore if you cannot get the maids or the young misses to assist you, e'en make short work and either singe or flay them; there is no great loss in the skins, and the flesh is just the same.

If you are employed in market, do not accept a treat of a beefsteak and a pot of ale from the butcher, which I think in conscience is no better than wronging your master, but do you always take that perquisite in money, if you do not go in trust, or in poundage when you pay the bills.

The kitchen bellows being usually out of order with stirring the fire with the muzzle to save tongs and poker, borrow the bellows out of your lady's bedchamber, which, being least used, are commonly the best in the house; and if you happen to damage or grease them, you have a chance to keep them entirely for your own use.

Let a blackguard-boy be always about the house to send on your errands and go to market for you in rainy days, which will save your clothes and make you appear more creditable to your mistress.

If your mistress allows you the kitchen-stuff, in return of her generosity, take care to boil and roast your meat sufficient. If she keeps it for her own profit, do her justice and rather than let a good fire be wanting, enliven it now and then with the dripping and the butter that happens to turn to oil.

Send up your meat well stuck with skewers to make it look round and plump; and an iron skewer, rightly employed now and then, will make it look handsomer.

When you roast a long joint of meat, be careful only about the middle and leave the two extreme parts raw, which may serve another time and will also save firing.

When you scour your plates and dishes, bend the brim inward so as to make them hold the more.

Always keep a large fire in the kitchen when there is a small dinner or the family dines abroad, that the neighbours, seeing the smoke, may commend your master's housekeeping, but when much company is invited, then be as sparing as possible of your coals, because a great deal of the meat, being half raw, will be saved and will serve for next day.

Boil your meat constantly in pump water, because you must sometimes want river or pipe water, and then your mistress, observing your meat of a different colour, will chide you when you are not in fault.

When you have plenty of fowl in the larder, leave the door open in pity to the poor cat, if she be a good mouser.

If you find it necessary to go to market in a wet day, take out your mistress' riding-hood and cloak to save your clothes.

Get three or four charwomen constantly to attend you in the kitchen, whom you pay at small charges, only with the broken meat, a few coals and all the cinders.

To keep troublesome servants out of the kitchen, always leave the winder sticking on the jack to fall on their heads.

If a lump of soot falls into the soup and you cannot conveniently get it out, scum it well, and it will give the soup a high French taste.

If you melt your butter to oil, be under no concern, but send it up, for oil is a genteeler sauce than butter.

Scrape the bottoms of your pots and kettles with a silver spoon, for fear of giving them a taste of copper.

When you send up butter for sauce, be so thrifty as to let it be half water, which is also much wholesomer.

Never make use of a spoon in anything that you can do with your hands, for fear of wearing out your master's plate.

When you find you cannot get dinner ready at the time appointed, put the clock back, and then it may be ready to a minute.

Let a red-hot coal now and then fall into the dripping-pan, that the smoke of the dripping may ascend and give the roast meat a high taste.

You are to look upon the kitchen as your dressing room, but you are not to wash your hands till you have gone to the necessary house, and spitted your meat, trussed your pullets, picked your salad, nor indeed till after you have sent up the second course, for your hands will be ten times fouled with the things you are forced to handle; but when your work is over, one washing will serve for all.

There is but one part of your dressing that I would admit while the victuals are boiling, roasting or stewing, I mean the combing your head, which loseth no time because you can stand over your cookery and watch it with one hand, while you are using your comb with the other.

If some of the combings happen to be sent up with the victuals, you may safely lay the fault upon any of the footmen that hath vexed you, as those gentlemen are sometimes apt to be malicious if you refuse them a sop in the pan or a slice from the spit, much more when you discharge a ladleful of hot porridge on their legs or send them up to their masters with a dish-clout pinned at their tails.

In roasting and boiling, order the kitchen-maid to bring none but the large coals, and save the small ones for the fires above stairs; the first are the properest for dressing meat, and when they are out, if you happen to miscarry in any dish, you may fairly lay the fault upon want of coals; besides, the cinder-pickers will be sure to speak ill of your master's housekeeping, where they do not find plenty of large cinders mixed with fresh large coals. Thus you may dress your meat with credit, do an act of charity, raise the honour of your master, and sometimes get a share of a pot of ale for your bounty to the cinder-woman.

As soon as you have sent up the second course, you have nothing to do in a great family until supper, therefore scour your hands and face, put on your hood and scarf, and take your pleasure among your cronies till nine or ten at night – but dine first.

Let there be always a strict friendship between you and the butler, for it is in both your interests to be united: the butler often wants a comfortable titbit, and you, much oftener, a cool cup of good liquor. However, be cautious of him, for he is sometimes an inconstant lover, because he hath great advantage to allure the maids with a glass of sack, or white wine and sugar.

When you roast a breast of veal, remember your sweetheart the butler loves a sweetbread, therefore set it aside till evening; you can say the cat or dog has run away with it, or you found it tainted, or fly-blown, and, besides, it looks as well on the table without the sweetbread as with it.

When you make the company wait long for dinner, and the meat be overdone (which is generally the case), you may lawfully lay the fault on your lady, who hurried you so to send up dinner, that you were forced to send it up too much boiled and roasted.

When you are in haste to take down your dishes, tip them in such a manner that a dozen will fall together upon the dresser, just ready for your hand.

To save time and trouble, cut your apples and onions with the same knife, for well-bred gentry love the taste of an onion in everything they eat.

Lump three or four pounds of butter together with your hands, then dash it against the wall just over the dresser, so as to have it ready to pull by pieces as you have occasion for it.

If you have a silver saucepan for kitchen use, let me advise you to batter it well and keep it always black; make room for the saucepan by wriggling it on the coals, etc. – this will be for your master's honour, because it shows there has been constant good housekeeping; and in the same manner, if you are allowed a large silver spoon for the kitchen, have the bowl of it be worn out with continual scraping and stirring, and often say merrily, 'This spoon owes my master no service.'

When you send up a mess of broth, water-gruel or the like to your master in a morning, do not forget with your thumb and two fingers to put salt on the side of the plate, for if you make use of a spoon or the end of a knife, there may be danger that the salt would fall, and that would be a sign of ill luck. Only remember to lick your thumb and fingers clean before you offer to touch the salt.

If your butter, when it is melted, tastes of brass, it is your master's fault, who will not allow you a silver saucepan; besides, the less of it will go further, and new tinning is very chargeable. If you have a silver saucepan and the butter smells of smoke, lay the fault upon the coals.

If your dinner miscarries in almost every dish, how could you help it? You were teased by the footmen coming into the kitchen, and, to prove it true, take occasion to be angry and throw a ladleful of broth on one or two of their liveries. Besides, Friday and Childermas-day are two cross days in the week, and it is impossible to have good luck on either of them, therefore on those two days you have a lawful excuse.

Directions to the Footman

Your employment, being of a mixed nature, extends to a great variety of business, and you stand in a fair way of being the favourite of your master and mistress, or of the young masters and misses. You are the fine gentleman of the family, with whom all the maids are in love. You are sometimes a pattern of dress to your master, and sometimes he is so to you. You wait at table in all companies, and consequently have the opportunity to see and know the world, and to understand men and manners. I confess your vails are but few, unless you are sent with a present, or attend a tea in the country, but you are called 'Mr' in the neighbourhood and sometimes pick up a fortune, perhaps your master's daughter, and I have known many of your tribe to have good commands in the army. In town you have a seat reserved for you in the playhouse, where you have an opportunity of becoming wits and critics. You have no professed enemy except the rabble and my lady's waiting-woman, who are sometimes apt to call you 'skip-kennel'[6]. I have a true veneration for your office, because I had once the honour to be one of your order, which I foolishly left by demeaning myself with accepting an employment in the Custom House. But that you, my brethren, may come to better fortunes, I shall here deliver my instructions, which have been the fruit of much thought and observation, as well as of seven years' experience.

In order to learn the secrets of other families, tell your brethren those of your master's; thus you will grow a favourite both at home and abroad, and regarded as a person of importance.

Never be seen in the streets with a basket or bundle in your hands, and carry nothing but what you can hide in your pocket, otherwise you will disgrace your calling, to prevent which, always retain a blackguard-boy to carry your loads, and, if you want farthings, pay him with a good slice of bread or scrap of meat.

Let a shoe-boy clean your own shoes first, for fear of fouling the chambers, and then let him clean your master's; keep him on purpose for that use and to run of errands, and pay him with scraps. When you are sent on an errand, be sure to hedge in some business of your own, either to see your sweetheart, or drink a pot of ale with your brother-servant, which is so much time clear gained.

There is a great controversy about the most convenient and genteel way of holding your plate at meals: some stick it between the frame and the back of the chair, which is an excellent expedient, where the make of the chair will allow it; others, for fear the plate should fall, grasp it so firmly that their thumb reacheth to the middle of the hollow, which, however, if your thumb be dry, is no secure method, and therefore in that case, I advise your wetting the bowl of it with your tongue. As to that absurd practice of letting the back of the plate lie leaning on the hollow of your hand, which some ladies recommend, it is universally exploded, being liable to so many accidents. Others, again, are so refined that they hold their plate directly under the left armpit, which is the best situation for keeping it warm, but this may be dangerous in the article of taking away a dish, where your plate may happen to fall upon some of the company's heads. I confess myself to have objected against all these ways, which I have frequently tried, and therefore I recommend a fourth, which is to stick your plate, up to the rim inclusive, in the left side between your waistcoat and your shirt; this will keep it at least as warm as your armpit – or ockster, as the Scots call it – this will hide it so as strangers may take you for a better servant, too good to hold a plate; this will secure it from falling, and, thus disposed, it lies ready for you to whip it out in a moment, ready warmed, to any guest within your reach who may want it. And, lastly, there is another convenience in this method, that if any time during your waiting you find yourselves going to cough or sneeze, you can immediately snatch out your plate and hold the hollow part close to your nose or mouth, and thus prevent spurting any moisture from either upon the dishes or the ladies' headdress. You see gentlemen and ladies observe a like practice on such an occasion with a hat or a handkerchief, yet a plate is less fouled and sooner cleaned than either of these, for, when your cough or sneeze is over, it is but returning your plate to the same position, and your shirt will clean it in the passage.

Take off the largest dishes and set them on with one hand, to show the ladies your vigour and strength of back, but always do it between two ladies, that if the dish happens to slip, the soup or sauce may fall on their clothes and not daub the floor. By this practice, two of our brethren, my worthy friends, got considerable fortunes.

Learn all the new-fashion words and oaths and songs and scraps of plays that your memory can hold. Thus you will become the delight of nine ladies in ten, and the envy of ninety-nine beaux in a hundred.

Take care that at certain periods, during dinner especially, when persons of quality are there, you and your brethren be all out of the room together, by which you will give yourselves some ease from the fatigue of waiting and, at the same time, leave the company to converse more freely, without being constrained by your presence.

When you are sent on a message, deliver it in your own words, although it be to a duke or a duchess, and not in the words of your master or lady, for how can they understand what belongs to a message as well as you, who have been bred to the employment? But never deliver the answer till it is called for, and then adorn it with your own style.

When dinner is done, carry down a great heap of plates to the kitchen, and when you come to the head of the stairs, trundle them all before you. There is not a more agreeable sight or sound, especially if they be silver, besides the trouble they save you, and there they will lie ready, near the kitchen door, for the scullion to wash them.

If you are bringing up a joint of meat in a dish, and it falls out of your hand, before you get into the dining room, with the meat on the ground and the sauce spilt, take up the meat gently, wipe it with the lap of your coat, then put it again into the dish and serve it up, and when your lady misses the sauce, tell her it is to be sent up in a plate by itself.

When you carry up a dish of meat, dip your fingers in the sauce, or lick it with your tongue to try whether it be good and fit for your master's table.

You are the best judge of what acquaintance your lady ought to have, and, therefore, if she sends you on a message of compliment or business to a family you do not like, deliver the message in such a manner as may breed a quarrel between them not to be reconciled; or, if a footman comes from the same family on the like errand, turn the answer she orders you to deliver in such a manner as the other family may take it for an affront.

When you are in lodgings, and no shoe-boy to be got, clean your master's shoes with the bottom of the curtains, a clean napkin, or your landlady's apron.

Ever wear your hat in the house but when your master calls, and as soon as you come into his presence, pull it off to show your manners.

Never clean your shoes on the scraper but in the entry or at the foot of the stairs, by which you will have the credit of being at home almost a minute sooner, and the scraper will last the longer.

Never ask leave to go abroad, for then it will be always known that you are absent, and you will be thought an idle rambling fellow, whereas, if you go out and nobody observes, you have a chance of coming home without being missed, and you need not tell your fellow-servants where you have gone, for they will be sure to say you were in the house but two minutes ago, which is the duty of all servants.

Snuff the candles with your fingers and throw the snuff on the floor, then tread it out to prevent stinking; this method will very much save the snuffers from wearing out. You ought also to snuff them close to the tallow, which will make them run and so increase the perquisite of the cook's kitchen-stuff, for she is the person you ought in prudence to be well with.

While grace is saying after meat, do you and your brethren take the chairs from behind the company, so that when they go to sit again they may fall backwards, which will make them all merry, but be you so discreet as to hold your laughter till you get to the kitchen, and then divert your fellow-servants.

When you know your master is most busy in company, come in and pretend to settle about the room, and, if he chides, say you thought he rung the bell. This will divert him from plodding on business too much, or spending himself in talk, or racking his thoughts, all which are hurtful to his constitution.

If you are ordered to break the claw of a crab or a lobster, clap it between the sides of the dining-room door between the hinges; thus you can do it gradually without mashing the meat, which is often the case by using the street-door key or the pestle.

When you take a foul plate from any of the guests, and observe the foul knife and fork lying on the plate, show your dexterity: take up the plate and throw off the knife and fork on the table without shaking off the bones or broken meat that are left; then the guest, who hath more time than you, will wipe the fork and knife already used.

When you carry a glass of liquor to any person who hath called for it, do not bob him on the shoulder, or cry, 'Sir, or madam, here's the glass'; that would be unmannerly, as if you had a mind to force it down one's throat; but stand at the person's right shoulder, and wait his time; and if he strikes it down with his elbow by forgetfulness, that was his fault and not yours.

When your mistress sends you for a hackney coach in a wet day, come back in the coach to save your clothes and the trouble of walking; it is better the bottom of her petticoats should be daggled with your dirty shoes than your livery be spoiled, and yourself get a cold.

There is no indignity so great to one of your station, as that of lighting your master in the streets with a lantern, and, therefore, it is very honest policy to try all arts how to evade it; besides, it shows your master to be either poor or covetous, which are the two worst qualities you can meet with in any service. When I was under these circumstances, I made use of several wise expedients, which I here recommend to you: sometimes I took a candle so long that it reached to the very top of the lantern and burnt it; but my master, after a good beating, ordered me to paste the top with paper. I then used a middling candle, but stuck it so loose in the socket that it leant towards one side and burnt a whole quarter of the horn. Then I used a bit of candle of half an inch, which sunk in the socket and melted the solder, and forced my master to walk half the way in the dark. Then he made me stick two inches of candle in the place where the socket was, after which I pretended to stumble, put out the candle, and broke all the tin part to pieces. At last he was forced to make use of a lantern-boy out of perfect good husbandry.

It is much to be lamented that gentlemen of our employment have but two hands to carry plates, dishes, bottles and the like out of the room at meals; and the misfortune is still the greater, because one of those hands is required to open the door while you are encumbered with your load. Therefore, I advise that the door may be always left ajar, so as to open it with your foot, and then you may carry out plates and dishes from your belly up to your chin, besides a good quantity of things under your arms, which will save you many a weary step; but take care that none of the burden falls until you are out of the room and, if possible, out of hearing.

If you are sent to the post office with a letter in a cold rainy night, step to the alehouse, and take a pot, until it is supposed you have done your errand, but take the next opportunity to put the letter in carefully, as becomes an honest servant.

If you are ordered to make coffee for the ladies after dinner, and the pot happens to boil over while you are running up for a spoon to stir it, or are thinking of something else, or struggling with the chambermaid for a kiss, wipe the sides of the pot clean with a dish-clout, carry up your coffee boldly, and when your lady finds it too weak, and examines you whether it hath not run over, deny the fact absolutely, swear you put in more coffee than ordinary, that you never stirred an inch from it, that you strove to make it better than usual because your mistress had ladies with her, that the servants in the kitchen will justify what you say. Upon this, you will find that the other ladies will pronounce your coffee to be very good, and your mistress will confess that her mouth is out of taste, and she will for the future suspect herself, and be more cautious in finding fault. This I would have you do from a principle of conscience, for coffee is very unwholesome, and, out of affection to your lady, you ought to give it her as weak as possible; and upon this argument, when you have a mind to treat any of the maids with a dish of fresh coffee, you may, and ought to subtract a third part of the powder on account of your lady's health, and getting her maids' goodwill.

If your master sends you with a small trifling present to one of his friends, be as careful of it as you would be of a diamond ring. Therefore, if the present be only half a dozen pippins, send up the servant who received the message to say that you were ordered to deliver them with your own hands. This will show your exactness and care to prevent accidents or mistakes, and the gentleman or lady cannot do less than give you a shilling. So when your master receives the like present, teach the messenger who brings it to do the same, and give your master hints that may stir up his generosity, for brother-servants should assist one another, since it is all for your master's honour, which is the chief point to be consulted by every good servant, and of which he is the best judge.

When you step but a few doors off to tattle with a wench, or take a running pot of ale, or to see a brother-footman going to be hanged, leave the street door open, that you may not be forced to knock and your master discover that you are gone out, for a quarter of an hour's time can do his service no injury.

When you take away the remaining pieces of bread after

dinner, put them on foul plates, and press them down with other plates over them, so as nobody can touch them; and so they will be a good perquisite to the blackguard-boy in ordinary.

When you are forced to clean your master's shoes with your own hand, use the edge of the sharpest case knife[7], and dry them with the toes an inch from the fire, because wet shoes are dangerous, and, besides, by these arts you will get them the sooner for yourself.

In some families the master often sends to the tavern for a bottle of wine, and you are the messenger. I advise you, therefore, to take the smallest bottle you can find, but, however, make the drawer give you a full quart, then you will get a good sup for yourself, and your bottle will be filled. As for a cork to stop it, you need be at no trouble, for the thumb will do as well, or a bit of dirty chewed paper.

In all disputes with chairmen and coachmen for demanding too much, when your master sends you down to chaffer with them, take pity of the poor fellows, and tell your master that they will not take a farthing less; it is more for your interest to get a share of a pot of ale than to save a shilling for your master, to whom it is a trifle.

When you attend your lady in a dark night, if she useth her coach, do not walk by the coach side, so as to tire and dirty yourself, but get up into your proper place behind it, and so hold the flambeau sloping forward over the coach roof, and when it wants snuffing, dash it against the corners.

When you leave your lady at church on Sundays, you have two hours safe to spend with your companions at the alehouse, or over a beefsteak and a pot of beer at home with the cook and the maids; and, indeed, poor servants have so few opportunities to be happy that they ought not to lose any.

Never wear socks when you wait at meals, on account of your own health as well as of them who sit at table, because, as most ladies like the smell of young men's toes, so it is a sovereign remedy against the vapours.

Choose a service, if you can, where your livery colours are least tawdry and distinguishing; green and yellow immediately betray your office, and so do all kinds of lace, except silver, which will hardly fall to your share, unless with a duke or some prodigal just come to his estate. The colours you ought to wish for are blue or filemot[8], turned up with red, which, with a borrowed sword, your master's linen, and a natural and improved confidence, will give you what title you please where you are not known.

When you carry dishes or other things out of the room at meals, fill both your hands as full as possible, for, although you may sometimes spill and sometimes let fall, yet you will find at the year's end, you have made great dispatch and saved abundance of time.

If your master or mistress happens to walk the streets, keep on one side, and as much on the level with them as you can, which people observing will either think you do not belong to them, or that you are one of their companions, but if either of them happen to turn back and speak to you, so that you are under the necessity to take off your hat, use but your thumb and one finger, and scratch your head with the rest.

In winter-time light the dining-room fire but two minutes before dinner is served up, that your master may see how saving you are of his coals.

When you are ordered to stir up the fire, clean away the ashes from between the bars with the fire brush.

When you are ordered to call a coach, although it be midnight, go no further than the door for fear of being out of the way when you are wanted, and there stand, bawling, 'Coach, coach,' for half an hour.

Although you gentlemen in livery have the misfortune to be treated scurvily by all mankind, yet you make a shift to keep up your spirits, and sometimes arrive at considerable fortunes. I was an intimate friend to one of our brethren, who was footman to a Court-lady: she had an honourable employment, was sister to an earl, and the widow of a man of quality. She observed something so polite in my friend, the gracefulness with which he tripped before her chair and put his hair under his hat, that she made him many advances, and one day taking the air in her coach with Tom behind it, the coachman mistook the way and stopped at a privileged chapel, where the couple were married, and Tom came home in the chariot by his lady's side. But he unfortunately taught her to drink brandy, of which she died, after having pawned all her plate to purchase it, and Tom is now a journeyman maltster.

Boucher, the famous gamester, was another of our fraternity, and when he was worth fifty thousand pounds he dunned the Duke of B***m for an arrear of wages in his service; and I could instance many more, particularly another, whose son had one of the chief employments at Court, and is sufficient to give you the following advice, which is to be pert and saucy to all mankind, especially to the chaplain, the waiting-woman and the better sort of servants in a person of quality's family, and value not now and then a kicking or a caning, for your insolence will at last turn to good account, and, from wearing a livery, you may probably soon carry a pair of colours.

When you wait behind a chair at meals, keep constantly wriggling the back of the chair, that the person behind whom you stand may know you are ready to attend him.

When you carry a parcel of china plates, if they chance to

fall, as it is a frequent misfortune, your excuse must be that a dog ran across you in the hall; that the chambermaid accidentally pushed the door against you; that a mop stood across the entry and tripped you up; that your sleeve stuck against the key or button of the lock.

When your master and lady are talking together in their bedchamber, and you have some suspicion that you or your fellow-servants are concerned in what they say, listen at the door for the public good of all the servants, and join all to take proper measures for preventing any innovations that may hurt the community.

Be not proud in prosperity. You have heard that fortune turns on a wheel; if you have a good place, you are at the top of the wheel. Remember how often you have been stripped and kicked out of doors; your wages are taken up beforehand and spent in translated red-heeled shoes, second-hand toupées, and repaired lace ruffles, besides a swingeing debt to the alewife and the brandy-shop. The neighbouring tapster, who before would beckon you over to a savoury bit of ox-cheek in the morning, give it to you gratis, and only score you up for the liquor, immediately after you were packed off in disgrace, carried a petition to your master to be paid out of your wages, whereof not a farthing was due, and then pursued you with bailiffs into every blind cellar. Remember how soon you grew shabby, threadbare and out at heels; was forced to borrow an old livery coat to make your appearance while you were looking for a place, and sneak to every house where you have an old acquaintance to steal you a scrap, to keep life and soul together, and, upon the whole, were in the lowest station of life, which, as the old ballad says, is that of a skip-kennel turned out of place. I say remember all this now, in your flourishing condition. Pay your contributions duly to your late brothers the cadets, who are left to the wide world; take one of them as your dependant to send on your lady's messages when you have a mind to go to the alehouse; slip him out privately now and then a slice of bread, and a bit of cold meat – your master can afford it; and if he be not yet put upon the establishment for a lodging, let him lie in the stable or the coach house, or under the back stairs, and recommend him to all the gentlemen who frequent your house as an excellent servant.

To grow old in the office of a footman is the highest of all indignities, therefore, when you find years coming on, without hopes of a place at Court, a command in the army, a succession to the stewardship, an employment in the Revenue (which two last you cannot obtain without reading and writing), or running away with your master's niece or daughter, I directly advise you to go upon the road, which is the only post of honour left you. There you will meet many of your old comrades, and live a short life and a merry one, and make a figure at your exit, wherein I will give you some instructions.

The last advice I will give you relates to your behaviour when you are going to be hanged, which, either for robbing your master, for house-breaking, or going upon the highway, or, in a drunken quarrel, by killing the first man you meet, may very probably be your lot, and is owing to one of these three qualities: either a love of good fellowship, a generosity of mind, or too much vivacity of spirits. Your good behaviour on this article will concern your whole community. At your trial deny the fact with all solemnity of imprecations; a hundred of your brethren, if they can be admitted, will attend about the bar and be ready upon demand to give you a good character before the court. Let nothing prevail on you to confess but a promise of pardon for discovering your comrades; but I suppose all this to be in vain, for, if you escape now, your fate will be the same another day. Get a speech to be written by the best author of Newgate; some of your kind wenches will provide you with a Holland shirt and white cap crowned with a crimson or black ribbon. Take leave cheerfully of all your friends in Newgate; mount the cart with courage; fall on your knees; lift up your eyes; hold a book in your hands although you cannot read a word; deny the fact at the gallows; kiss and forgive the hangman, and so farewell. You shall be buried in pomp, at the charge of the fraternity; the surgeon shall not touch a limb of you, and your fame shall continue until a successor of equal renown succeeds in your place.

Directions to the Coachman

You are strictly bound to nothing but to step into the box, and carry your master or lady.

Let your horses be so well trained that, when you attend your lady at a visit, they will wait until you slip into a neighbouring alehouse to take a pot with a friend.

When you are in no humour to drive, tell your master that the horses have got a cold, that they want shoeing, that rain does them hurt and roughens their coat and rots the harness. This may likewise be applied to the groom.

If your master dines with a country friend, drink as much as you can get, because it is allowed that a good coachman never drives so well as when he is drunk, and then show your skill by driving to an inch by a precipice, and say you never drive so well as when drunk.

If you find any gentleman fond of one of your horses and willing to give you a consideration beside the price, persuade your master to sell him, because he is so vicious that you cannot undertake to drive with him, and is foundered into the bargain.

Get a blackguard-boy to watch your coach at the church door on Sundays, that you and your brother-coachmen may be merry together at the alehouse, while your master and lady are at church.

Take care that your wheels be good, and get a new set bought as often as you can, whether you are allowed the old as your perquisite or not. In one case it will turn to your honest profit, and in the other it will be a just punishment on your master's covetousness, and probably the coach-maker will consider you too.

Directions to the Groom

You are the servant upon whom the care of your master's honour in all journeys entirely depends: your breast is the sole repository of it. If he travels the country and lodges at inns, every dram of brandy, every pot of ale extraordinary that you drink raiseth his character, and, therefore, his reputation ought to be dear to you, and I hope you will not stint yourself in either. The smith, the saddler's journeyman, the cook at the inn, the ostler and the boot catcher, ought all, by your means, to partake of your master's generosity; thus his fame will reach from one county to another, and what is a gallon of ale or a pint of brandy in His Worship's pocket? And although he should be in the number of those who value their credit less than their purse, yet your care of the former ought to be so much the greater. His horse wanted two removes; your horse wanted nails; his allowance of oats and beans was greater than the journey required; a third part may be retrenched and turned into ale or brandy, and thus his honour may be preserved by your discretion, and less expense to him; or, if he travels with no other servant, the matter is easily made up in the bill between you and the tapster.

Therefore, as soon as you alight at the inn, deliver your horses to the stable-boy, and let him gallop them to the next pond; then call for a pot of ale, for it is very fit that a Christian should drink before a beast. Leave your master to the care of the servants in the inn, and your horses to those in the stable; thus both he and they are left in the properest hands. But you are to provide for yourself; therefore get your supper, drink freely and go to bed without troubling your master, who is in better hands than yours. The ostler is an honest fellow, loves horses in his heart, and would not wrong the dumb creatures for the world. Be tender of your master, and order the servants not to wake him too early. Get your breakfast before he is up, that he may not wait for you; make the ostler tell him the roads are very good and the miles short, but advise him to stay a little longer until the weather clears up, for he is afraid there will be rain, and he will be time enough after dinner.

Let your master mount before you, out of good manners. As he is leaving the inn, drop a good word in favour of the ostler, what care he took of the cattle; and add that you never saw civiller servants. Let your master ride on before, and do you stay until the landlord hath given you a dram, then gallop after him through the town or village with full speed, for fear he should want you, and to show your horsemanship.

If you are a piece of a farrier, as every good groom ought to be, get sack, brandy or strong beer to rub your horse's heels every night, and be not sparing, for (if any be spent) what is left, you know how to dispose of it.

Consider your master's health, and, rather than let him take long journeys, say the cattle are weak and fallen in their flesh with hard riding; tell him of a very good inn five miles nearer than he intended to go, or leave one of his horse's foreshoes loose in the morning, or contrive that the saddle may pinch the beast in his withers, or keep him without corn all night and morning, so that he may tire on the road, or wedge a thin plate of iron between the hoof and the shoe to make him halt, and all this in perfect tenderness to your master.

When you are going to be hired, and the gentleman asks whether you are apt to be drunk, own freely that you love a cup of good ale, but that it is your way, drunk or sober, never to neglect your horses.

When your master hath a mind to ride out for the air, or

for pleasure, if any private business of your own makes it inconvenient for you to attend him, give him to understand that the horses want bleeding or purging; that his own pad hath got a surfeit; or that the saddle wants stuffing and his bridle is gone to be mended. This you may honestly do, because it will be no injury to the horses or your master, and at the same time shows the great care you have of the poor dumb creatures.

If there be a particular inn in the town whither you are going, and where you are well acquainted with the ostler or tapster and the people of the house, find fault with the other inns, and recommend your master thither; it may probably be a pot and a dram or two more in your way, and to your master's honour.

If your master sends you to buy hay, deal with those who will be most liberal to you, for, service being no inheritance, you ought not to let slip any lawful and customary perquisite. If your master buys it himself, he wrongs you, and, to teach him his duty, be sure to find fault with that hay as long as it lasts, and if the horses thrive with it, the fault is yours.

Hay and oats, in the management of a skilful groom, will make excellent ale as well as brandy, but this I only hint.

When your master dines, or lies at a gentleman's house in the country, although there be no groom, or he be gone abroad, or that the horses have been quite neglected, be sure to employ one of the servants to hold the horse when your master mounts. This I would have you do when your master only alights to call in for a few minutes, for brother-servants must always befriend one another, and this also concerns your master's honour because he cannot do less than give a piece of money to him who holds his horse.

In long journeys ask your master leave to give ale to the

horses; carry two quarts full to the stable, pour half a pint into a bowl, and if they will not drink it, you and the ostler must do the best you can. Perhaps they may be in a better humour at the next inn, for I would have you never fail to make the experiment.

When you go to air your horses in the park, or the fields give them to a horse-boy, or one of the blackguards, who, being lighter than you, may be trusted to run races with less damage to the horses, and teach them to leap over hedges and ditches while you are drinking a friendly pot with your brother-grooms. But sometimes you and they may run races yourselves for the honour of your horses and of your masters.

Never stint your horses at home in hay and oats, but fill the rack to the top and the manger to the brim, for you would take it ill to be stinted yourself, although, perhaps, they may not have the stomach to eat; consider, they have no tongues to ask. If the hay be thrown down, there is no loss, for it will make litter and save straw.

When your master is leaving a gentleman's house in the country, where he hath lain a night, then consider his honour: let him know how many servants there are, of both sexes, who expect vails, and give them their cue to attend in two lines as he leaves the house; but desire him not to trust the money with the butler, for fear he should cheat the rest. This will force your master to be more generous, and then you may take occasion to tell your master, that Squire Such-a-one, whom you lived with last, always gave so much apiece to the common servants, and so much to the housekeeper and the rest, naming at least double to what he intended to give, but be sure to tell the servants what a good office you did them; this will gain you love, and your master honour.

You may venture to be drunk much oftener than the

coachman, whatever he pretends to allege in his own behalf, because you hazard nobody's neck but your own, for the horse will probably take so much care of himself as to come off with only a strain or a shoulder-slip.

When you carry your master's riding-coat in a journey, wrap your own in it and buckle them up close with a strap, but turn your master's inside out to preserve the outside from wet and dirt; thus, when it begins to rain, your master's coat will be first ready to be given to him, and, if it get more hurt than yours, he can afford it better, for your livery must always serve its year's apprenticeship.

When you come to your inn with the horses wet and dirty after hard riding, and are very hot, make the ostler immediately plunge them into water up to their bellies and allow them to drink as much as they please, but be sure to gallop them full-speed a mile at least, to dry their skins and warm the water in their bellies. The ostler understands his business, leave all to his discretion while you get a pot of ale and some brandy at the kitchen fire to comfort your heart.

If your horse drop a foreshoe, be so careful as to alight and take it up, then ride with all the speed you can (the shoe in your hand that every traveller may observe your care) to the next smith on the road. Make him put it on immediately, that your master may not wait for you, and that the poor horse may be as short a time as possible without a shoe.

When your master lies at a gentleman's house, if you find the hay and oats are good, complain aloud of their badness; this will get you the name of a diligent servant; and be sure to cram the horses with as much oats as they can eat while you are there, and you may give them so much the less for some days at the inns, and turn the oats into ale. When you leave the gentleman's house, tell your master what a covetous huncks that gentleman was, that you got nothing but buttermilk or water to drink; this will make your master out of pity allow you a pot of ale more at the next inn; but, if you happen to get drunk in a gentleman's house, your master cannot be angry, because it cost him nothing, and so you ought to tell him as well as you can in your present condition, and let him know it is both for his and the gentleman's honour to make a friend's servant welcome.

A master ought always to love his groom, to put him into a handsome livery, and to allow him a silver-laced hat. When you are in this equipage, all the honours he receives on the road are owing to you alone; that he is not turned out of the way by every carrier, is caused by the civility he receives at second hand from the respect paid to your livery.

You may now and then lend your master's pad to a brother-servant, or your favourite maid, for a short jaunt, or hire him for a day, because the horse is spoiled for want of exercise, and if your master happens to want his horse, or hath a mind to see the stable, curse that rogue the helper who is gone out with the key.

When you want to spend an hour or two with your companions at the alehouse, and that you stand in need of a reasonable excuse for your stay, go out of the stable door, or the back way, with an old bridle, girth or stirrup leather in your pocket, and on your return, come home by the street-door with the same bridle, girth, or stirrup leather dangling in your hand, as if you came from the saddler's, where you were getting the same mended; if you are not missed all is well, but if you are met by your master, you will have the reputation of a careful servant. This I have known practised with good success.

Directions to the House Steward and Land Steward

Lord Peterborough's steward that pulled down his house, sold the materials, and charged my lord with repairs. Take money for forbearance from tenants. Renew leases and get by them, and sell woods. Lend my lord his own money. (Gil Blas said much of this, to whom I refer.[9])

Directions to the Porter

If your master be a minister of state, let him be at home to none but his pimp, or chief flatterer, or one of his pensionary writers, or his hired spy and informer, or his printer in ordinary, or his city solicitor, or a land-jobber, or his inventor of new funds, or a stockjobber.

Directions to the Chambermaid

The nature of your employment differs according to the quality, the pride or the wealth of the lady you serve, and this treatise is to be applied to all sorts of families, so that I find myself under great difficulty to adjust the business for which you are hired. In a family where there is a tolerable estate, you differ from the housemaid, and in that view I give my directions. Your particular province is your lady's chamber, where you make the bed and put things in order, and if you live in the country, you take care of rooms where ladies lie who come into the house, which brings in all the vails which fall to your share. Your usual lover, as I take it, is the coachman, but if you are under twenty and tolerably handsome, perhaps a footman may cast his eyes on you.

Get your favourite footman to help you in making your lady's bed, and if you serve a young couple, the footman and you, as you are turning up the bedclothes, will make the prettiest observations in the world, which, whispered about, will be very entertaining to the whole family, and get among the neighbourhood.

Do not carry down the necessary vessels for the fellows to see, but empty them out of the window, for your lady's credit. It is highly improper for menservants to know that fine ladies have occasion for such utensils; and do not scour the chamber pot, because the smell is wholesome.

If you happen to break any china with the top of the whisk on the manteltree or the cabinet, gather up the fragments, put them together as well as you can, and place them behind the rest, so that when your lady comes to discover them, you may safely say they were broke long ago, before you came to the service. This will save your lady many an hour's vexation.

It sometimes happens that a looking glass is broken by the same means, while you are looking another way; as you sweep the chamber, the long end of the brush strikes against the glass and breaks it to shivers. This is the extremest of all misfortunes, because it is impossible to be concealed. Such a fatal accident once happened in a great family where I had the honour to be a footman, and I will relate the particulars to show the ingenuity of the poor chambermaid on so sudden and dreadful an emergency, which perhaps may help to sharpen your invention if your evil star should ever give you the like occasion. The poor girl had broken a large Japan glass of great value with a stroke of her brush; she had not considered long when, by a prodigious presence of mind, she locked the door, stole into the yard, brought a stone of three-pound weight into the chamber, laid it on the hearth just under the looking glass, then broke a pane in the sash window that looked into the same yard, so shut the door, and went about her other affairs. Two hours after, the lady goes into the chamber, sees the glass broken, the stone lying under, and a whole pane in the window destroyed, from all which circumstances she concluded, just as the maid could have wished, that some idle straggler in the neighbourhood, or perhaps one of the out-servants, had, through malice, accident or carelessness, flung in the stone and done the mischief. Thus far all things went well, and the girl concluded herself out of danger, but it was her ill fortune that a few hours after in came the parson of the parish, and the lady (naturally) told him the accident, which you may believe had much discomposed her. But the minister, who happened to understand mathematics, after examining the situation of the yard, the window and the chimney, soon convinced the lady that the stone could never reach the looking glass without taking three turns in its flight from the hand that threw it, and the maid, being proved to have swept the room the same morning, was strictly examined, but constantly denied that she was guilty upon her salvation, offering to take her oath upon the Bible before his Reverence that she was innocent as the child unborn; yet the poor wench was turned off, which I take to have been hard treatment, considering her ingenuity. However, this may be a direction to you in the like case, to contrive a story that will better hang together. For instance, you might say that while you were at work with the mop or brush, a flash of lightning came suddenly in at the window, which almost blinded you; that you immediately heard the ringing of broken glass on the hearth; that, as soon as you recovered your eyes, you saw the looking glass all broken to pieces; or you may allege that observing the glass a little covered with dust, and going very gently to wipe it, you suppose the moisture of the air had dissolved the glue or cement, which made it fall to the ground; or, as soon as the mischief is done, you may cut the cords that fastened the glass to the wainscot, and so let it fall flat on the ground, run out in a fright, tell your lady, curse the upholsterer, and declare how narrowly you escaped that it did not fall upon your head. I offer these expedients from a desire I have to defend the innocent, for innocent you certainly must be if you did not break the glass on purpose, which I would by no means excuse, except upon great provocations.

Oil the tongs, poker and fire shovel up to the top, not only to keep them from rusting, but likewise to prevent meddling people from wasting your master's coals with stirring the fire.

When you are in haste, sweep the dust into a corner of the room, but leave your brush upon it, that it may not be seen, for that would disgrace you.

Never wash your hands, or put on a clean apron, until you have made your lady's bed, for fear of rumpling your apron or fouling your hands again.

When you bar the window-shuts of your lady's bedchamber at nights, leave open the sashes to let in the fresh air and sweeten the room against morning.

In the time when you leave the windows open for air, leave books or something else on the window-seat, that they may get air too.

When you sweep your lady's room, never stay to pick up foul smocks, handkerchiefs, pinners, pin-cushions, teaspoons, ribbons, slippers or whatever lieth in your way, but sweep all into a corner, and then you may take them up in a lump and save time.

Making beds in hot weather is a very laborious work, and you will be apt to sweat; therefore, when you find the drops running down from your forehead, wipe them off with a corner of the sheet, that they may not be seen on the bed.

When your lady sends you to wash a china cup, and it happen to fall, bring it up, and swear you did but just touch it with your hand when it broke into *three halves*; and here I must inform you, as well as your fellow-servants, that you ought never to be without an excuse; it doth no harm to your master and it lessens your fault, as in this instance. I do not condemn you for breaking the cup; it is certain you did not break it on purpose, and the thing is possible that it might break in your hand.

You are sometimes desirous to see a funeral, a quarrel, a man going to be hanged, a wedding, a bawd carted or the like. As they pass by in the street, you lift up the sash suddenly; there by misfortune it sticks. This was no fault of yours; young women are curious by nature; you have no remedy but to cut the cord and lay the fault upon the carpenter, unless nobody saw you, and then you are as innocent as any servant in the house.

Wear your lady's smock when she has thrown it off; it will do you credit, save your own linen, and be not a pin the worse.

When you put a clean pillowcase on your lady's pillow, be sure to fasten it well with three corking-pins, that it may not fall off in the night.

When you spread bread and butter for tea, be sure that all the holes in the loaf be left full of butter to keep the bread moist against dinner, and let the mark of your thumb be seen only upon one end of every slice, to show your cleanliness.

When you are ordered to open or lock any door, trunk or cabinet, and miss the proper key, or cannot distinguish it in the bunch, try the first key that you can thrust in, and turn it with all your strength until you open the lock or break the key, for your lady will reckon you a fool to come back and do nothing.

Directions to the Waiting-maid

Two accidents have happened to lessen the comforts and profits of your employment: first, that execrable custom got among ladies of trucking their old clothes for china, or turning them to cover easy chairs, or making them into patchwork for screens, stools, cushions and the like. The second is the invention of small chests and trunks with lock and key, wherein they keep the tea and sugar, without which it is impossible for a waiting-maid to live, for, by this means, you are forced to buy brown sugar, and pour water upon the leaves when they have lost all their spirit and taste. I cannot contrive any perfect remedy against either of these two evils. As to the former, I think there should be a general confederacy of all the servants in every family, for the public good, to drive those china hucksters from the doors; and as to the latter, there is no other method to relieve yourselves but by a false key, which is a point both difficult and dangerous to compass, but as to the circumstance of honesty in procuring one, I am under no doubt, when your mistress gives you so just a provocation, by refusing you an ancient and legal perquisite. The mistress of the teashop may now and then give you half an ounce, but that will only be a drop in the bucket, therefore I fear you must be forced, like the rest of your sisters, to run in trust, and pay for it out of your wages, as far as they will go, which you can easily make up other ways if your lady be handsome or her daughters have good fortunes.

If you are in a great family, and my lady's woman, my lord may probably like you, although you are not half so handsome as his own lady. In this case, take care to get as much out of him as you can, and never allow him the smallest liberty, not the squeezing of your hand, unless he puts a guinea into it; so, by degrees, make him pay accordingly for every new attempt, doubling upon him in proportion to the concessions you allow, and always struggling and threatening to cry out or tell your lady, although you receive his money. Five guineas for handling your breast is a cheap pennyworth, although you seem to resist with all your might, but never allow him the last favour under a hundred guineas, or a settlement of twenty pounds a year for life.

In such a family, if you are handsome, you will have the choice of three lovers: the chaplain, the steward, and my lord's gentleman. I would first advise you to choose the steward, but if you happen to be young with child by my lord, you must take up with the chaplain. I like my lord's gentleman the least of the three, for he is usually vain and saucy from the time he throws off his livery, and if he misseth a pair of colours or a tidewaiter's place, he hath no remedy but the highway.

I must caution you particularly against my lord's eldest son. If you are dextrous enough, it is odds that you may draw him in to marry you and make you a lady, if he be a common rake or a fool (and he must be one or the other), but if the former, avoid him like Satan, for he stands in less awe of a mother than my lord doth of a wife, and, after ten thousand promises, you will get nothing from him but a big belly or a clap – and probably both together.

When your lady is ill, and, after a very bad night, is getting a little nap in the morning, if a footman comes with a message to enquire how she doth, do not let the compliment be lost, but shake her gently until she wakes, then deliver the message, receive her answer, and leave her to sleep.

If you are so happy as to wait on a young lady with a great fortune, you must be an ill manager if you cannot get five or six hundred pounds for disposing of her. Put her often in mind that she is rich enough to make any man happy; that there is no real happiness but in love; that she hath liberty to choose wherever she pleaseth, and not by the direction of parents, who never give allowances for an innocent passion; that there are a world of handsome, fine, sweet young gentlemen in town, who would be glad to die at her feet; that the conversation of two lovers is a heaven upon earth; that love like death equals all conditions; that if she should cast her eyes upon a young fellow below her in birth and estate, his marrying her would make him a gentleman; that you saw yesterday on the Mall the prettiest ensign, and that if you had forty thousand pounds, it should be at his service. Take care that everybody should know what lady you live with, how great a favourite you are, and that she always takes your advice. Go often to St James's Park; the fine fellows will soon discover you, and contrive to slip a letter into your sleeve or your bosom. Pull it out in a fury and throw it on the ground, unless you find at least two guineas along with it, but, in that case, seem not to find it, and to think he was only playing the wag with you. When you come home, drop the letter carelessly in your lady's chamber; she finds it, is angry; protest you knew nothing of it, only you remember that a gentleman in the park struggled to kiss you, and you believe it was he that put the letter in your sleeve or petticoat, and, indeed, he was as pretty a man as she ever saw; that she may burn the letter if she pleaseth. If your lady be wise, she will burn some other paper before you, and read the letter when you are gone down. You must follow this practice as often as you safely can, but let him who pays you best with every letter be the handsomest man. If a footman presumes to bring a letter to the house to be delivered to you for your lady, although it come from your best customer, throw it at his head; call him impudent rogue and villain, and shut the door in his face; run up to your lady, and, as a proof of your fidelity, tell her what you have done.

I could enlarge very much upon this subject, but I trust to your own discretion.

If you serve a lady who is a little disposed to gallantries, you will find it a point of great prudence how to manage. Three things are necessary: first, how to please your lady; secondly, how to prevent suspicion in the husband or among the family; and lastly, but principally, how to make it most for your advantage. To give you full directions in this important affair would require a large volume. All assignations at home are dangerous, both to your lady and yourself, and therefore contrive as much as possible to have them in a third place, especially if your lady, as it is a hundred odds, entertains more lovers than one, each of whom is often more jealous than a thousand husbands, and very unlucky rencounters may often happen under the best management. I need not warn you to employ your good offices chiefly in favour of those whom you find most liberal, yet if your lady should happen to cast an eye upon a handsome footman, you should be generous enough to bear with her humour, which is no singularity, but a very natural appetite. It is still the safest of all home intrigues, and was formerly the least suspected, until of late years it hath grown more common. The great danger is lest this kind of gentry, dealing too often in bad ware, may happen not to be sound, and then your lady and you are in a very bad way, although not altogether desperate.

But, to say the truth, I confess it is a great presumption in me to offer you any instructions in the conduct of your lady's amours, wherein your whole sisterhood is already so expert and deeply learned, although it be much more difficult to compass than that assistance which my brother-footmen give their masters on the like occasion, and, therefore, I leave this affair to be treated by some abler pen.

When you lock up a silk mantua, or laced head in a trunk or chest, leave a piece out that, when you open the trunk again, you may know where to find it.

Directions to the Housemaid

If your master and lady go into the country for a week or more, never wash the bedchamber or dining room until just the hour before you expect them to return. Thus the rooms will be perfectly clean to receive them, and you will not be at the trouble to wash them so soon again.

I am very much offended with those ladies who are so proud and lazy that they will not be at the pains of stepping into the garden to pluck a rose[10], but keep an odious implement, sometimes in the bedchamber itself, or at least in a dark closet adjoining, which they make use of to ease their worst necessities; and you are the usual carriers-away of the pan, which maketh not only the chamber, but even their clothes offensive to all who come near. Now, to cure them of this odious practice, let me advise you – on whom this office lies to convey away this utensil – that you will do it openly, down the great stairs, and in the presence of the footmen; and, if anybody knocks, to open the street door while you have the vessel filled in your hands. This, if anything can, will make your lady take the pains of evacuating her person in the proper place, rather than expose her filthiness to all the menservants in the house.

Leave a pail of dirty water with the mop in it, a coal-box, a bottle, a broom, a chamber pot, and such other unsightly things, either in a blind entry or upon the darkest part of the back stairs, that they may not be seen, and if people break their shins by trampling on them, it is their own fault.

Never empty the chamber pots until they are quite full. If that happens in the night, empty them into the street, if in the morning, into the garden, for it would be an endless work to go a dozen times from the garret and upper rooms down to the backsides; but never wash them in any other liquor except their own; what cleanly girl would be dabbling in other folk's urine? And, besides, the smell of stale, as I observed before, is admirable against the vapours, which, a hundred to one, may be your lady's case.

Brush down the cobwebs with a broom that is wet and dirty, which will make them stick the faster to it, and bring them down more effectually.

When you rid up the parlour hearth in a morning, throw the last night's ashes into a sieve, and what falls through, as you carry it down, will serve instead of sand for the room and the stairs.

When you have scoured the brasses and the irons in the parlour chimney, lay the fouled wet clout upon the next chair, that your lady may see you have not neglected your work. Observe the same rule when you clean the brass locks, only with this addition: to leave the marks of your fingers on the doors, to show you have not forgot.

Leave your lady's chamber pot in the bedchamber window all day to air.

Bring up none but large coals to the dining room and your lady's chamber; they make the best fires, and if you find them too big, it is easy to break them on the marble hearth.

When you go to bed, be sure take care of fire, and therefore blow the candle out with your breath and then thrust it under your bed. *Note:* the smell of the snuff is very good against vapours.

Persuade the footman who got you with child to marry you before you are six months gone, and if your lady asks you why you would take a fellow who was not worth a groat, let your answer be that service is no inheritance.

When your lady's bed is made, put the chamber pot under it, but in such a manner as to thrust the valance along with it, that it may be full in sight and ready for your lady when she hath occasion to use it.

Lock up a cat or a dog in some room or closet, so as to make such a noise all over the house as may frighten away the thieves, if any should attempt to break or steal in.

When you wash any of the rooms towards the street overnight, throw the foul water out of the street door, but be sure not to look before you, for fear those on whom the water lights might think you uncivil, and that you did it on purpose. If he who suffers breaks the windows in revenge, and your lady chides you and gives positive orders that you should carry the pail down and empty it in the sink, you have an easy remedy. When you wash an upper room, carry down the pail so as to let the water dribble on the stairs all the way down to the kitchen, by which not only your load will be lighter, but you will convince your lady that it is better to throw the water out of the windows, or down the street-door steps. Besides, this latter practice will be very diverting to you and the family in a frosty night, to see a hundred people falling on their noses or backsides before your door when the water is frozen.

Polish and brighten the marble hearths and chimney-pieces with a clout dipped in grease; nothing makes them shine so well, and it is the business of the ladies to take care of their petticoats.

If your lady be so nice that she will have the room scoured with freestone, be sure to leave the marks of the freestone six inches deep round the bottom of the wainscot, that your lady may see your obedience to her orders.

Directions to the Dairymaid

Fatigue of making butter; put scalding water in your churn, although in summer, and churn close to the kitchen fire, and with cream of a week old. Keep cream for your sweetheart.

Directions to the Children's Maid

If a child be sick, give it whatever it wants to eat or drink, although particularly forbid by the doctor, for what we long for in sickness will do us good; and throw the physic out of the window; the child will love you the better, but bid it not tell. Do the same to your lady when she longs for anything in sickness, and engage it will do her good.

If your mistress comes to the nursery and offers to whip a child, snatch it out of her hands in a rage, and tell her she is the cruellest mother you ever saw. She will chide, but love you the better. Tell the children stories of spirits when they offer to cry, etc.

Be sure to wean the children, etc.

Directions to the Nurse

If you happen to let the child fall, and lame it, be sure never confess it; and if it dies, all is safe.

Contrive to be with child as soon as you can while you are giving suck, that you may be ready for another service when the child you nurse dies, or is weaned.

Directions to the Laundress

If you singe the linen with the iron, rub the place with flour, chalk or white powder, and if nothing will do, wash it so long till it be either not to be seen or torn to rags. Always wash your own linen first.

About tearing linen in washing.

When your linen is pinned on the line or on a hedge and it rains, whip it off, although you tear it, etc. But the place for hanging them is on young fruit trees, especially in blossom; the linen cannot be torn, and the trees give them a fine smell.

Directions to the Housekeeper

You must always have a favourite footman whom you can depend upon, and order him to be very watchful when the second course is taken off, that it be brought safely to your office, that you and the steward may have a titbit together.

Directions to the Tutoress or Governess

Say the children have sore eyes; Miss Betty won't take to her book, etc.

Make the misses read French and English novels and French romances, and all the comedies writ in King Charles II and King William's reigns, to soften their nature and make them tender-hearted, etc.

NOTES

1. From the late sixteenth century, a preliminary detention centre for debtors.
2. A chamber pot.
3. Tips.
4. 'White friars' is a dialect term for a flake or particle of white scum or froth floating on liquid.
5. Provisions, or food.
6. A common term in the seventeenth century for a footman or lackey.
7. A case knife is a large kitchen or table knife.
8. A yellowish-brown colour, literally the colour of dead leaves.
9. Probably a reference to the tremendously popular picaresque novel, *L'Histoire de Gil Blas de Santillane* [*Gil Blas*] (1715–35) written by Alain-René LeSage (1668–1747) and translated (or rather adapted) into English by Tobias Smollett (1721–71) in 1749.
10. An archaic slang term meaning 'to urinate', used especially of women.

NOTE ON THE TEXT

As pointed out by the publisher, George Faulkner, in his introduction to the 1752 edition of *Directions to Servants*, Swift did not finish off the work and left it slightly unpolished as he wished to devote his time to more serious and useful works. Apparently Swift intended to write a much longer work, and did not have the energies or the inspiration to complete it. This explains the somewhat sketchy nature of some passages. The current text is based on the 1746 edition (also published in Dublin by G. Faulkner), but we have also availed ourselves of the 1745 edition (published in London by R. Dodsley & M. Cooper) and the 1964 Pantheon Books edition.

BIOGRAPHICAL NOTE

Jonathan Swift was born in Dublin in 1667, into an Anglo-Irish Protestant family. His father died before Swift was born and his mother returned to her own family in England, leaving her son in the care of relatives. Swift received a good education in Kilkenny and later at Trinity College, Dublin.

After completing his degree, Swift moved for the first time to England, and, in 1689, he became secretary to Sir Willian Temple at Moor Park in Surrey. Here he met and fell in love with Esther Johnson, the 'Stella' of his journal. He visited Ireland briefly in 1690, but returned to England the following year, where he was awarded a degree from Oxford University in 1692. At about this time, Swift published his first poem; it did not meet with critical acclaim and his attempts to achieve a position in the Church of England were likewise unsuccessful, and in 1694 he returned once again to Ireland.

In 1695, Swift was finally ordained as an Anglican priest and given the small prebendary of Kilroot. He remained there for less than a year, however, and in 1696 returned to Moor Park. Here he began to write some of his greatest works, including the religious satire *A Tale of a Tub*, and *The Battle of the Books*, a satire defending the works of the 'Ancients' against those of the 'Moderns'; both remained unpublished until 1704. In 1699 Temple died, and again Swift returned to Ireland, where he was appointed vicar of Laracor.

Swift continued to visit England, and became involved with Whig politics, writing several political pamphlets. His loyalties shifted, however, in 1707, when the Whigs dismissed his request for a remission of Irish clerical taxation, and in 1710 he became editor of the Tory newspaper *The Examiner*.

Swift became a founder member of the Scriblerus Club in

1714, a satirical literary group whose members also included Alexander Pope, John Arbuthnot, John Gay and Thomas Parnell, and whose influence was significant in Swift's own later work. Later the same year, however, the Tories fell from power and Swift was forced to return to Ireland for good, where he was installed as Dean of St Patrick's Cathedral in Dublin. He continued to produce satires and pamphlets, and rose to become a heroic figure in his native land with works such as *Drapier's Letters* (1724), protesting about English monopolies, and *A Modest Proposal* (1729), a savagely ironic work in which he suggested that the problem of the Irish famine could be solved if the Irish resorted to eating their own children.

Swift's most famous work, *Gulliver's Travels*, was published in 1726. It was a hugely successful social satire, though now largely regarded as a children's book, and demonstrated his intense and growing pessimism at what he perceived as the follies of mankind. His final years were filled with illness and bitterness; his mental state was almost certainly deteriorating from the 1730s onwards, and, in 1742, he suffered a stroke which left him in need of permanent care. In 1745, Swift died and was buried in St Patrick's Cathedral.

HESPERUS PRESS – 100 PAGES

Hesperus Press, as suggested by the Latin motto, is committed to bringing near what is far – far both in space and time. Works written by the greatest authors, and unjustly neglected or simply little known in the English-speaking world, are made accessible through new translations and a completely fresh editorial approach. Through these short classic works, each around 100 pages in length, the reader will be introduced to the greatest writers from all times and all cultures.

For more information on Hesperus Press, please visit our website: **www.hesperuspress.com**

ET REMOTISSIMA PROPE

SELECTED TITLES FROM HESPERUS PRESS

Author	*Title*	*Foreword writer*
Pietro Aretino	*The School of Whoredom*	Paul Bailey
Jane Austen	*Love and Friendship*	Fay Weldon
Honoré de Balzac	*Colonel Chabert*	A.N. Wilson
Charles Baudelaire	*On Wine and Hashish*	Margaret Drabble
Giovanni Boccaccio	*Life of Dante*	A.N. Wilson
Charlotte Brontë	*The Green Dwarf*	Libby Purves
Mikhail Bulgakov	*The Fatal Eggs*	Doris Lessing
Giacomo Casanova	*The Duel*	Tim Parks
Miguel de Cervantes	*The Dialogue of the Dogs*	
Anton Chekhov	*The Story of a Nobody*	Louis de Bernières
Wilkie Collins	*Who Killed Zebedee?*	Martin Jarvis
Arthur Conan Doyle	*The Tragedy of the Korosko*	Tony Robinson
William Congreve	*Incognita*	Peter Ackroyd
Joseph Conrad	*Heart of Darkness*	A.N. Wilson
Gabriele D'Annunzio	*The Book of the Virgins*	Tim Parks
Dante Alighieri	*New Life*	Louis de Bernières
Daniel Defoe	*The King of Pirates*	Peter Ackroyd
Marquis de Sade	*Incest*	Janet Street-Porter
Charles Dickens	*The Haunted House*	Peter Ackroyd
Fyodor Dostoevsky	*Poor People*	Charlotte Hobson
Joseph von Eichendorff	*Life of a Good-for-nothing*	
George Eliot	*Amos Barton*	Matthew Sweet
F. Scott Fitzgerald	*The Rich Boy*	John Updike
Gustave Flaubert	*Memoirs of a Madman*	Germaine Greer
E.M. Forster	*Arctic Summer*	Anita Desai
Ugo Foscolo	*Last Letters of Jacopo Ortis*	Valerio Massimo Manfredi
Elizabeth Gaskell	*Lois the Witch*	Jenny Uglow

Théophile Gautier	*The Jinx*	Gilbert Adair
André Gide	*Theseus*	
Nikolai Gogol	*The Squabble*	Patrick McCabe
Thomas Hardy	*Fellow-Townsmen*	Emma Tennant
Nathaniel Hawthorne	*Rappaccini's Daughter*	Simon Schama
E.T.A. Hoffmann	*Mademoiselle de Scudéri*	Gilbert Adair
Victor Hugo	*The Last Day of a Condemned Man*	Libby Purves
Joris-Karl Huysmans	*With the Flow*	Simon Callow
Henry James	*In the Cage*	Libby Purves
Franz Kafka	*Metamorphosis*	Martin Jarvis
Heinrich von Kleist	*The Marquise of O–*	Andrew Miller
D.H. Lawrence	*The Fox*	Doris Lessing
Leonardo da Vinci	*Prophecies*	Eraldo Affinati
Giacomo Leopardi	*Thoughts*	Edoardo Albinati
Nikolai Leskov	*Lady Macbeth of Mtsensk*	Gilbert Adair
Niccolò Machiavelli	*Life of Castruccio Castracani*	Richard Overy
Katherine Mansfield	*In a German Pension*	Linda Grant
Guy de Maupassant	*Butterball*	Germaine Greer
Herman Melville	*The Enchanted Isles*	Margaret Drabble
Francis Petrarch	*My Secret Book*	Germaine Greer
Luigi Pirandello	*Loveless Love*	
Edgar Allan Poe	*Eureka*	Sir Patrick Moore
Alexander Pope	*Scriblerus*	Peter Ackroyd
Alexander Pushkin	*Dubrovsky*	Patrick Neate
François Rabelais	*Pantagruel*	Paul Bailey
François Rabelais	*Gargantua*	Paul Bailey
Friedrich von Schiller	*The Ghost-seer*	Martin Jarvis
Percy Bysshe Shelley	*Zastrozzi*	Germaine Greer
Stendhal	*Memoirs of an Egotist*	Doris Lessing

Robert Louis Stevenson	*Dr Jekyll and Mr Hyde*	Helen Dunmore
Theodor Storm	*The Lake of the Bees*	Alan Sillitoe
Italo Svevo	*A Perfect Hoax*	Tim Parks
W.M. Thackeray	*Rebecca and Rowena*	Matthew Sweet
Leo Tolstoy	*Hadji Murat*	Colm Tóibín
Ivan Turgenev	*Faust*	Simon Callow
Mark Twain	*The Diary of Adam and Eve*	John Updike
Giovanni Verga	*Life in the Country*	Paul Bailey
Jules Verne	*A Fantasy of Dr Ox*	Gilbert Adair
Edith Wharton	*The Touchstone*	Salley Vickers
Oscar Wilde	*The Portrait of Mr W.H.*	Peter Ackroyd
Virginia Woolf	*Carlyle's House*	Doris Lessing
Virginia Woolf	*Monday or Tuesday*	Scarlett Thomas
Emile Zola	*For a Night of Love*	A.N. Wilson